MW00930986

Clean Water

by Kathy Furgang

Houghton Mifflin Harcourt™

ISBN: 978-0-544-07360-9

13 14 15 16 17 18 19 20   1083   20 19 18

4500710511   B C D E F G

Contents

Vocabulary

mixture

density

solution

Stretch Vocabulary

reservoirs   wastewater

aquifer   distillation

filtration

Introduction

When you turn on the faucet at home, you take for granted that water will be there for you when you need it. But your water has gone through a complex process to get to you.

Most of Earth's water is ocean water. It has salt in it and can't normally be used in our homes for drinking or bathing. Freshwater accounts for only about 2% of Earth's water supply, and much of that water is frozen in glaciers. So even though Earth is known as the water planet, very little of the world's water can actually be used for our water needs.

Read on to find out how the water you use at home is collected, cleaned, and delivered to you.

Our communities depend on a reliable supply of clean, fresh water.

Water, Water, Everywhere!

We need water to stay alive, but where does our water come from? We rely on the water cycle. The water on Earth's surface is constantly being recycled. Water is found in oceans, rivers, lakes, and streams. As the water heats and evaporates from oceans, it condenses and falls as rain. This rain can be collected in reservoirs, or large lakes used as water-supply sources. Reservoirs can be natural or human-made.

Depending on where you live, your drinking water might come from a reservoir, or it might come from an underground source called an aquifer. An aquifer is an area of underground rock. This rock collects water that seeps underground through

Reservoirs collect rainwater. The water must go through a cleansing process.

the soil or through breaks in the rock. In times of heavy rain, reservoirs and aquifers may be full. In times of dry weather, there is a lot less water available from these water sources.

The water that collects in reservoirs and aquifers is freshwater. But this freshwater is not actually *clean* water. There can be many pollutants or bacteria in the water. We can't drink it right out of the reservoirs or aquifers because it could make us sick. The water that we drink must meet safety laws called standards. Without these safety standards in place, people could get very sick from drinking unclean water.

What kind of unsafe ingredients are in freshwater before it is cleaned for us to drink? Some of the contaminants in water occur naturally in the environment, such as bacteria or other organisms. However, some contaminants are human-made, such as pollution: chemicals, waste, and other toxins. That's why systems are set up to collect the water, bring it to a facility, and clean the water before it can be used. Modern systems and new technologies help scientists come up with the best ways to clean large amounts of water. This clean water can then be used by millions of people who need it in nearby cities and towns, as well as in very remote areas where fewer people live.

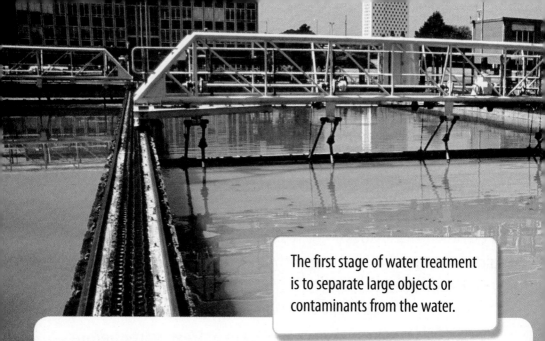

The first stage of water treatment is to separate large objects or contaminants from the water.

Clean It Up

A water treatment plant is the place where water gets cleaned and prepared for distribution. The process of cleaning the water involves removing contaminants that are mixed into the water. A mixture is a combination of two or more different substances in which the substances keep their identities. Water first arrives at a water treatment plant as a mixture of water, rocks, mud, sticks, and other materials. It is the job of the treatment plant to separate the mixture so that only the water remains. This process takes several steps. This kind of mixture is separated by using screens and filters, the same way that many other mixtures are separated.

Screens rise up through the water and separate out large chunks. Sticks, rocks, and even garbage are pulled away and out of the mixture. These objects can be found all throughout the mixture. Some sink to the bottom, while others float to the top, depending on their densities. Objects such as rocks are denser than water, so they will sink. Objects such as empty aluminum cans are less dense than water. They will float to the top before the screens are even used.

If solids are found in the water, they keep their original properties in the mixture. They can easily be removed by the screens. However, sometimes harmful chemicals are found in the water. These will remain in the water until later in the process. The first step removes only large chunks from the water. Chemicals that are dissolved in the water will be removed later in the process.

After the first step of the filtering process, the water may still not be clear and it will certainly not be safe to drink. It will go through more filtering and cleaning at the water treatment plant.

Some water treatment plants can process almost four hundred million liters of water in a single day. These numbers are especially high in the summer, when people use more water.

Clean Some More

The next step in the water treatment process is to send the water through even more filters. The smaller the holes on the filters and screens, the smaller the objects that are separated from the mixture. The screens eventually become so small that particles only one millionth of an inch can be removed. That's a thorough mixture separation! However, the separation must be that thorough. Any small contaminant could affect the health of the person who drinks the water. Water treatment is important for the safety of the whole community. The water must be tested at each stage to make sure that the process is working correctly.

Chlorine and water are mixed together to form a solution.

After the filtering process, there are still dissolved substances in the water. The water is a solution. In a solution, unlike a mixture, different substances are evenly mixed, and the resulting combination has the same composition throughout. The water is tested for certain chemicals to make sure that there are not enough of them to be harmful. But some chemicals are added, too. Very small amounts of a chemical called chlorine are added to the water to kill bacteria and other organisms that cannot be removed by filtering. Now the water is ready to drink!

After the solution is mixed, the water is sent on its way to communities to be used. Large systems of pipes bring the water from the treatment plant to cities and towns. Extra water supplies are often kept in large storage tanks before they are distributed. From here, more pipes move the water into homes and businesses. The mixture that comes into a water treatment plant is very different from the solution that leaves it.

It's Dirty Again

When we use water, it can become pretty dirty! We use water to clean ourselves and to clean things in our homes, and we use it to wash away waste of all kinds. We put detergents and other cleaners into water. This used, dirty water goes into drains. Industries can also make water extremely dirty. Chemicals used in factory processes may get into the water supply. These chemicals can be harmful to humans, animals, plants, and soil.

Water that has been used is called wastewater, or sewage. Wastewater is routed through pipes to a wastewater treatment plant. This is a plant where sewage is cleaned and then put back into the water supply. It is different from a water treatment plant.

The process at a wastewater treatment plant is even more complex than the work done at water treatment plants. While freshwater will have some contaminants in it, the sewage-contaminated water is much more harmful; it is completely unusable when it is sent to the treatment plant.

The first thing that is done in a wastewater treatment plant is to remove large solids from the water. Next, the water goes to huge tanks where bacteria eat, or consume, organisms and other organic materials in the water. The bacteria added to the sewage work very quickly to break down the organic matter in the dirty water.

Then, the water goes to more tanks, where oxygen is added to the water. This process helps to separate out more materials from the water. Tiny materials settle to the bottom of the tanks where they can be collected. Then the water returns to tanks, where more bacteria remove the pollutants that might be left. These processes are repeated several times to be sure that the water becomes clean.

Chemical tests are performed at each stage to determine what kinds of pollutants and other harmful materials might still remain in the water. At each stage of the wastewater treatment process, the water becomes cleaner.

This wastewater leaves a factory where it was used in industrial processes. The water must be cleaned before it is recycled.

The water is tested for harmful substances before it is returned, through a large system of pipes, to the community to be used.

Ready for the Trip Back

Water that comes out of the wastewater treatment plant may go back into the environment, or it may be reused in other ways. But first, the water is treated with chlorine. Just as in the water treatment plants, the chlorine is added in very small amounts. Once the chlorine is added, it spreads evenly throughout the water, forming a solution.

Treated water is tested to make sure it is safe before it leaves the treatment plant. Treated water is used for many different purposes, including watering crops and golf courses. However, this water is not sent back to homes to be used.

Many wastewater plants, like water treatment plants, are set up so that millions of liters of water can pass through them each day. That's a lot of water! Some chemical processes for cleaning water must be ruled out because of their costs. One method, called distillation, can be used to clean liquids. Distillation is a process in which a solution is boiled. The gas is collected and cooled through condensation, producing a pure liquid. Distillation is able to get rid of many kinds of contaminants in water. This process is even used to make ocean saltwater clean enough to drink. Because of its cost, however, distilling saltwater is only done in parts of the world where there is no other way to get clean drinking water.

Distillation processes are also used in other kinds of factories to clean liquids. Factories that make fuels, medicines, and some drinks use distillation. However, the process is too expensive to be used in most wastewater treatment plants.

Scientists are always looking for new ways to separate mixtures or to clean unsafe solutions in order to make them safe again. Perhaps in your lifetime there will be easier, less expensive methods to clean water.

Keep Water Clean!

Not all water you come into contact with goes through a treatment plant. Lakes, rivers, and groundwater may contain pollutants. Some of these pollutants are particularly dangerous. For example, lead, mercury, and other substances called heavy metals are toxic. They are natural materials, but they are not needed or used by organisms. In fact, they can cause deadly diseases in humans as well as in other animals and plants that rely on water to live.

Most organisms on Earth depend on water to live. Clean water supports life, but toxic water can destroy it. That is why it is essential to keep Earth's water supplies as clean as possible.

The fish we catch and eat should be living in clean water.

Research Your Water Supply

Find out where your local water comes from. Research it in your local library or on the Internet. Find out how the water is collected and where it goes to be treated both before and after it is used. Report your findings to the class.

Write an Opinion

Write an opinion letter to a local newspaper explaining why it is important to keep local water systems clean. Discuss how water treatment plants work to solve water pollution problems and what problems they cannot help with. Read your letter to the class.

Glossary

aquifer [AW·kwe·fir] Area of underground rock that collects water that seeps underground.

density [DEN·sih·tee] The mass of an object based on the object's volume.

distillation [dis·til·A·shun] Process in which a liquid is heated and cooled in order to make it clean.

filtration [FIL·tray·shun] Process that involves separating large pieces from a mixture.

mixture [MIKS·cher] A combination of two or more different substances in which the substances keep their identities.

reservoir [rez·ur·VWAR] Large lake used as a source of water supply.

solution [suh·LOO·shuhn] A mixture that has the same composition throughout because all the parts are mixed evenly.

wastewater [WAYST·wah·tur] Water that has been used and must be cleaned and recycled.